D0840169

A Quilt for Elizabeth

by Benette W. Tiffault

illustrated by Mary McConnell

*Additional copies
may be ordered from:*
Centering Corporation
1531 N. Saddle Creek Road
Omaha, Nebraska 68104
(402) 553-1200

Ever since I was a baby, we lived in a cozy little house with a great big front porch and a tree house around back my daddy built in our apple tree.

Mommy said she laughed when he started to build it because babies can't play in tree houses. But he told her I would grow and it would be there for me.

When I was eight years old, my Daddy got very sick and he had to stay in the hospital for a long time. At dinner, Daddy's chair seemed like a very empty place. And it took me longer to fall asleep at night because he wasn't there to scratch my back.

Whenever I could, I went to the hospital with Mommy to see Daddy. I drew lots of pictures for his room to help him feel more comfortable. Because Daddy and I loved to go fishing together, I made him a special mobile out of a wire coat hanger and string, and we hung it over his bed. It had paper fish with eyes made out of tiny shells and yarn dangling down to look like seaweed. It was my own idea, and Daddy loved it.

On Daddy's birthday, the nurses let us bring a cake to his room. We made him a chocolate cake with cream cheese frosting because that was his favorite. When Mommy lit the candles, I pretended we were all at home in our kitchen singing "Happy Birthday," while Grandma played along with us on the piano. The house would be decorated with balloons and streamers, and Daddy's eyes would be bright and happy.

Then I remembered where we were.

"Why do we have to be here?" I shouted. "I don't want to come here anymore! Not ever again!" I was mad about everything, but when I looked at Daddy's face and knew what I had said, I felt terrible and started to cry. How could I ever hurt Daddy?

"Come sit next to me, honey," Daddy said.

"I'm sorry, Daddy," I said looking down at the floor. A big part of me wanted to disappear.

"Elizabeth, I understand you are angry at my illness, and not at me," he said softly. "I know that you love me. I really do." I was so happy he knew my feelings; I burst into tears and he hugged me tight.

"There are times when I get upset, too," he said. "Sometimes I feel angry and sad to think that I may not be here to see you grow up. But then I feel so lucky that I'm your daddy, and I wouldn't change that for anything."

"I do love you, Daddy," I said as I put my arms around him. Daddy held me close for a long time, and I wanted him to never let go.

Early one morning, Mommy came into my room and told me that Daddy had died. She said that his body was so tired and sick that it couldn't work anymore, and now the pain he had been feeling was gone.

I lay on my bed, hiding my face in my pillow. Mommy put her hand on my back and rubbed it gently.

"I don't believe you!" I said as I sat up in bed. "Daddy lives here. He should come home!"

"Daddy can't come home today or ever," Mommy said. "I know it's very hard, but I will try to help you understand as best I can."

"I don't want to understand!" I said. "I just want Daddy to come home!"

Then I cried and cried until my pillow was all wet with tears, and my mommy rubbed my back the whole time.

"How far away is Daddy?" I asked my mommy one day when I was wondering about everything.

"Daddy is inside you and inside me, and inside Grandma and inside everyone else who loved him, way down deep in our hearts," she said as she held me close to her. "Whenever we think about Daddy, it's kind of like holding his hand."

That made me feel better.

It was summertime, so I spent most days playing with my friends. But sometimes at the end of the day, I liked to go to my tree house by myself to sink deep into my bean bag chair and think about things. As daylight faded, I would search through darkening branches for the first star, and when it came out, I believed Daddy was watching it, too.

Often that summer, I ate dinner at my grandma's house. I went there through my own secret path that went behind my tree house, through our rock garden, and between some loose boards in our fence.

One night, Grandma made macaroni and cheese because she knew it was my favorite. We usually washed the dishes together after eating, but tonight she said, "Elizabeth, come here, I have something to show you."

I sat close to Grandma as she squeezed my hand and rested it on her soft dress. Then she reached beside the sofa, taking hold of a large hat box tied with a satin ribbon.

As she untied the bow she said, "I've been thinking. I believe you're ready to learn how to sew. We can start by stitching together these pieces of fabric."

To my surprise, Grandma had saved dozens of swatches of material from our old clothes—the ones we loved so much we'd worn them until our skin showed through.

As I picked up the square on top of the pile and rubbed it gently against my cheek, I closed my eyes and remembered Daddy's plaid flannel shirt. I could picture Daddy wearing that shirt while splitting wood for our fireplace last winter. After we stacked it into a tall pile by our house, we sat and warmed together by the fire.

Grandma said I could start with that piece.

With a silvery needle and golden thread, I stitched
it to a calico patch saved from the dress I had worn
to my fifth birthday party. That year, Daddy gave me
a jewelry box he had found at a flea market.
Everything felt magical as I lifted the lid and watched
a ballerina dance.

Grandma reached down deep in the box and pulled out a piece of faded denim.

"Your dad tore those jeans the first time he wore them," she said. "He got himself stuck on top of a fence when he was being chased by a neighbor's dog. We needed a ladder to get him down!"

We laughed together at the thought of it.

In the middle of the pile were large gray woolen pockets saved from my father's old bathrobe. I held both pockets in my hands and remembered how Daddy would hide a butterscotch in one of them, and I tried to guess where it was. The scent of the wintergreen soap Daddy always used came from the pockets and seemed to fill me up. As tears spilled from my eyes, Grandma used the pockets to dry them. When I was ready, she guided my hands, and together we sewed the pockets to the quilt.

Next, I chose a checkered square from the pile. Grandma told me we had eaten dozens of cookies and spilled many glasses of milk upon that cloth when it covered her kitchen table.

"When your Daddy was a little boy," she said, "his favorite cookies were oatmeal with grape jelly centers."

For a moment, Grandma stopped and put her hands to her eyes.

"You know," I said, "they're my favorite, too!" Then, she looked at me and smiled.

Night after night, Grandma and I pieced together the quilt. As it took form, we remembered times spent with my father, her son.

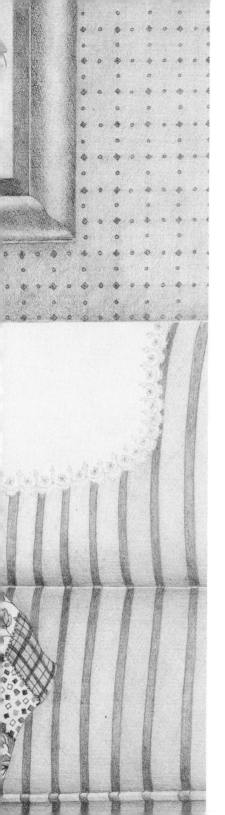

Around Thanksgiving, we finished making the quilt. As Grandma and I looked at it proudly, I noticed how our tiny stitches now held together the once separate squares. It was then I realized that memories of my father were also threaded tightly within me, so nothing could ever really take him away.

The next morning, I climbed the ladder to my tree house while holding the quilt close to me as if it were a baby. When I reached the top, the crisp winds rustling the leaves below made me shiver, so I wrapped the quilt tightly around me like a cocoon. Then, I put my hand deep in Daddy's pocket, stitched so carefully to the border, and found a butterscotch I had hidden inside.

And there I was, high within my tree house, snug beneath the quilt, and feeling better about everything as the butterscotch melted sweetly, and slowly disappeared.

To Families & Friends...

At any age, it is one of life's greatest challenges to try to understand and cope with the death of a loved one. If your child should experience the loss of someone she or he dearly loved, you may wonder how you might ease the child's passage through the grieving process.

It is hoped that **A Quilt for Elizabeth** will help you open up a healing dialogue about separation and loss with your child. In simple terms, it shows how her loving grandmother helps Elizabeth come to terms with feelings following her father's death. As she discovers that he continues to be with her in memory, Elizabeth acquires a greater sense of herself and of her father's spiritual presence in her life.

A child who hears this story may also be comforted knowing that it is understandable and appropriate to experience a wide range of emotions—from anger, to resentment, to guilt, to denial, to loneliness, to acceptance, to eventually feeling better.

It may be best to hold your child close and read **A Quilt for Elizabeth** together for the first time. That way, you can warmly comfort your child by answering any questions that arise, and by sharing your own special memories with each other.

This book is dedicated to the children of Kathleen Jaquin (Jennifer, Erin, and Katie), and to the children of Joseph Peppone (Luke, Nicholas, and Hannah).

Thank you to Joy Johnson, C.W. Pike, and Kimlee Butterfield for their guidance.